TRIGGER

TRIGGER

C. G. MOORE

Little Island

Books create waves

TRIGGER

First published in 2024 by
Little Island Books
7 Kenilworth Park
Dublin 6W
Ireland

A British Library Cataloguing in Publication record for this book
is available from the British Library.

Cover by Jack Smyth
Typeset by Rosa Devine
Printed in Poland by L&C

Print ISBN: 978-1-915071-53-8
Ebook ISBN: 978-1-915071-58-3

Little Island has received funding to support this book from the
Arts Council of Ireland / An Chomhairle Ealaíon

10 9 8 7 6 5 4 3 2 1

For Jake
for pushing me to be the best
version of myself

AUTHOR'S FOREWORD

Trigger covers some issues that cut deep and hit really close to home. I was sexually assaulted twice. For a long time, I had an inexplicable feeling of shame whenever I thought about it. I got out alive so why was I harping on about it? Why was I making myself out to be a victim? But the trauma from those nights has formed a layer that stays with me, and impacts on me, to this day. I have to constantly remind myself that I did not put myself into these situations expecting this to happen. I was, and am, a victim. I have learnt to accept that. It happened and I need to be kind to myself because recovering from this is difficult enough as it is without fighting myself at every turn.

Consent is so important and I don't see many stories that open and facilitate discussion around it. I don't think we discuss consent enough in the media and I wanted to write a story that will hopefully encourage candid conversations around abuse and sexual assault, destigmatise it and allow us to learn how we can support other survivors.

Although I have experienced sexual assault, I am not the best person to give advice or discuss any trauma you may have experienced. I would actively encourage you to report any incidents of this kind directly to the police and to use some of the resources listed at the end of this book.

Remember, you are not alone. Help is always just around the corner (even if you can't see it!)

PART 1

Survival

HOLLOW

I don't remember
Anything from that night.

I don't remember
How I got
The bruises down my thighs.

I don't remember
How I woke up there,
Wet grass splayed around me.

I don't remember
When they scooped out
All of me
From this hollow husk
Of a body.

THE PARK

Head heavy,
Lifeless limbs,
Muddled mind –
Every sound
Slices through my being,
A waterfall of sensations
Drowning me.

I feel for my phone,
Fingertips grazing the cracks.
Hold down the power button.

Nothing.

A golf ball
Whizzes overhead.
I get to my feet,
Stumble into tree cover,
Face drenched in sweat,
Dried blood and
Fresh tears.

SUNRISE

I emerge from the trees
To a ball of blazing red
Setting the Sunday skyline
On fire.

Bones aching,
Body beaten,
Mind battered,
I wonder how something
So beautiful
Can exist
When I'm
So lost?

WET

I traipse through the park,
Avoiding Sunday-morning joggers.
I glance around me,
Dip a hand in my bottoms.

I examine the slick liquid,
Burning bright
Against pale skin.

BLOOD

Blood looks so alluring,
So sexualised and seductive
In TV and film.

Blood –
It soaks through my clothes,
Shines a light
On secrets that will not
Reveal themselves to me.

ARE YOU OK?

Are you OK?

The question catches me off-guard.
A girl –
She must be sixteen?
Dressed for a shift
At Sandra's Deli.

Are you OK?

I notice honey-blond streaks
In her light-brown hair,
The single-heart earring,
The ruby-red lipstick –
Too glam for a morning shift
At the deli.
Are you OK?

Am I OK?
What is OK?

Babe?
Are you OK?
Want me to call someone?

My eyes answer:
Salty tears on broken skin.

I'M HERE NOW

I see Lau
Through blurred vision.
His hands hug me close –
The world stops spinning.

His fingers squeeze
My shoulder blades
While he tells me,
I'm here now.

But where is Jackson?
Why didn't he pick up?

JACKSON

Jackson was with me
In the club.
I need him –
His hugs,
His kisses,
The hot chocolate he makes me
With clouds of whipped cream
Trying to escape the mug
Just like Mum's.
I need Jackson
Here with me now.

NOBODY

Lau pats my back,
Asking questions
A mile
A minute.

I search my brain
For answers –
Draw blanks.

If that girl hadn't called him,
Where would I be now?

No phone.
No money.
No ID.

Nobody.

SHADOW

My memory is fuzzy.
The details
Of last night are
Cloaked in shadow.

I try to remember,
Shine a light
Into the darkness,
But it's no use.

Wisps of memories
Escape my grasp,
Swim out of reach,
Dissolve in darkness.

WHERE ARE WE?

Lau pulls up
Outside A&E.
I fold my arms,
Dig my feet
Into the footwell.

You need to get checked.

I know he's right,
Know that I need
To understand
Why there is blood
In my briefs,
Why there are bruises
Covering my body,
Why I cannot remember
What happened last night.

I lock the door,
Fold my arms –
Unsure if I am ready
To hear what must be said.

LAU

Lau was quiet.
I was dramatic.

Lau was there
When the boys tore me down.

Lau helped me navigate
The schoolyard minefield.

Lau's calm affected me,
Let me breathe through the pain.

Lau's friendship held me up,
Helped me survive high school.

Every day of high school:
Survival.

BEST FRIENDS

I met Lau in high school.
After I came out.
He asked me
If I wanted to hang out
After school.
I let my fingers linger
On the bruises
Forming under my school uniform
Before I accepted.

We went to the bowling alley,
Played game after game.
Lau walked me home,
Right to the door.
I leaned in
For the kiss.
Lau pulled away.
*We don't have to kiss
Just because we're gay,*
He told me.

We love each other
As friends.
We've been best friends
Ever since.

TRIAGE

The triage nurse
Asks questions,
Notes my answers.

He takes my temperature,
Measures my blood pressure.

He presses down on the bruises,
Asks me if it hurts,
Tells me to rate the pain.

One is nothing,
Ten is agony.

My body is a five,
My mind is a ten.
Finally,
I have an answer for the girl
Who works at Sandra's Deli:
I am not OK.

PAIN

Pain isn't just
A physical sensation
Affecting nerve and tissue.

Pain isn't just
A gashed knee
Or a broken bone.

Pain can be impacted by
Emotional,
Social,
Psychological factors –
Not *just physical pain*.

My pain is a ten,
Physical sensation dimming
Under jagged thoughts
Hacking away at my memories.

WISH

I wish Mum were here.

When I was seven,
I fractured my arm
Falling off the monkey bars.
Mum scooped me up,
Held me close,
Waited while the doctors
Inspected the damage.
She made everything OK.

On the drive home,
We ate chips in the car,
Steam clouding the windows,
Enveloping us in our own bubble.

THE FACE

Shaped like an egg,
Etchings of hair
Around nose and mouth.

Dark eyes
Cloaking emotion.

The palest skin
You ever did see –
Milk white.

A mouth that could
Swallow the world.

For the first time,
I see *him.*

DO YOU WANT TO DRAW HIM?

Lau worries I'll forget
The finer details,
But every inch
Of that man's face is
Branded in my brain
Every time
I close my eyes.

UNIFORMS

I'm sitting
In a hard-backed chair,
Hyperaware of the sounds
Around me –
Beeping machines,
The flush of a toilet,
Squeaky footsteps.

I try to focus
On breathing.
The uniforms
Approach me,
Guided by my nurse.

Can we talk?

QUESTION

The question isn't:
Can we talk?
But rather:
Can *I* talk?

Will words form,
Make their way
From larynx to mouth,
Fill up this room with sound?

ARROWS

Do you remember ...

Where you were?
Their faces?
How many people?
The time?
Date?
Location?
What you were doing before?
Who you were with?

Questions rain
On me
Like arrows.

SHAME AND SCORN

I sit outside
The interview room,
Waiting –
Always waiting.

So much silence
Swimming around me,
Filling me
With shame and scorn.

COLLECTING SAMPLES

I follow commands:

Open your mouth.
Lift your gown.
Lie on your back.

The nurse collects samples:
Of blood and saliva.

I am more than the blood
Flowing through my veins.
I live with the knowledge
Of something I can almost touch
But might never know.

SEXUAL ASSAULT UNIT

They assess the injuries,
Probe my bruises.

They reassure me that
This will be OK.

No one can promise that.

COLONOSCOPY

They think it's a surface wound
That will heal itself,
But they need to be sure.

They hand me a white pill –
It will relax me
For the enema.

I wish Jackson was here
To hold my hand.

ENEMA

Tears gather
As soon as they touch me.

Tears cascade
Down my face
As they show me
The enema:
Lift my gown,
Force it inside.

I scream,
Shards of emotion and memories
Intensifying the pain
In my mind.

Hands press down on me,
Holding me still –
While pain ripples
Through me.

ENTRAPMENT

It feels like something is
Forcing the oxygen from my lungs
As they strap the mask
Tightly over nose and mouth.

The clinical smell
Shrouds me like a veil,
Quelling the thoughts
Fizzing inside my head.

STATS

Stats helps me understand
Why this might have happened,
What help there is and
Why I am feeling like this.

They tell me that sixty per cent
Of male survivors are
Raped by someone they know –
Twenty-five per cent of rapes are
By a partner or ex-partner.

They can't tell me
Who did this to me and
Although they offer
Maybes and possibilities,
I need definites.
I need to know
The who and the why.
I can't dismantle my anger
Until I have answers.

MY MIND

my mind
moves slowly
from one thought
to the next

there's a man
lying in the bed
next to me

he looks angelic,
so serene
as he sleeps.

is that how I looked
while I slept?

THE WEIGHT OF REALITY

Mum and Dad are waiting
By the front door.

I open the door –
I run into Mum's arms.

The weight of reality
Hits me like Thor's hammer.

The doctor thinks I was ...

Mum holds me closer –
I never want to let go.

SLEEP

I sleep with the lights on,
Frightened by the secrets
Held by the darkness.

I sleep with the curtains open,
A window of escape
Ready when I need it.

I sleep with hands clenched,
Grip tightening around my lamp,
Ready to attack.

HURT

I cannot hurt a nightmare,
Bruise it like the men
That bruised me.

I cannot hurt a memory,
Rip it apart like the men
That tore my clothes apart.

I cannot hurt a thought,
Discard it like the men
That discarded me after use.

They.
Will.
Pay.

RIVER

Did Jackson think I was a river?
Rapid waters
Carving out their own path
Across the land.

Did he think me capable
Of re-shaping the world around me?
A force of nature
Yet to meet an unmovable object.

Does he think
I am strong enough
To survive this
Alone?

SOMETIMES

Sometimes I scare myself
When I'm lying in bed,
Stray thoughts
Wandering the maze
Of my mind.

I think about life.
I think about death.
I think of all the things that
Have been.
I think of all the things that
Might never be.
I feel everything.
I feel nothing.

I scare myself.
Sometimes.

SEPARATION

I separate body and mind
Marring memories
Divisions blurring
When pain fizzes
Into a hornets' nest
Of sensation.

I separate me from myself
When clothes come off
Panic building
When eyes settle on skin
Looking at a body
That is not my own.

HONEY AND GLASS

Sweeter than honey
The boy before
Door open
Living his life
What is his future?
Filled with fructose
He enchants you.

Sharper than glass
The boy after
Walls up
Struggling to survive
What is his past?
Cold to the touch
He frightens you.

PART 2

The New Normal

QUESTIONS

Lau doesn't tell me
Where we are going,
But I don't ask.

Usually,
I like to be in control,
Like to know
The wheres,
The whats,
The whys.

Right now,
All my questions
Concern that night.

Where was Jackson?
What did they do to me?
Why did they do it?

I tap my fingers
Against the dashboard,
Bite the inside
Of my lip,
As the city skyline
Disappears in the rear-view mirror.

MEMORY I

Dad chased me
Into hungry waves.

Mum bought me
A bucket and spade.

We sat for hours,
Constructing a sandcastle neighbourhood.

I carried a bucket of water,
Splashed it over the sandcastles.

I watched as the water
Erased any trace we'd been to the seaside.

Like we never were.

SEASIDE

I sit
On a tropical-coloured towel.

Knees drawn close,
I watch the waves.

They're wild,
Like my thoughts.

The wind whips my hair
Around my face.

Why can I remember things
That happened
Twelve years ago
　　　　　　　But not that night?

MEMORY II

Jackson took me to the seaside
A month before *that night.*

We rode the waltzers
Until I hurled.

We counted the lights
Like they were stars.

We felt the cool breeze
At the top of the Ferris wheel.

We were invincible.
I was happy.

MELODY

I stare at the messages
Read but not answered.

Is it me
Or is it Jackson?

Does he blame himself
For what happened?

I look at my dialled numbers:
A love letter to Jackson.

Jackson is a melody
I can't forget.

SWEET ESCAPE

When I swim,
I focus on breathing,
On hands slicing the water
And legs paddling to stay afloat.

I dive in,
One with the water.
My body comes alive,
Every muscle working in unison.

Half-formed memories
Enter my mind.
It takes a split second
But the waves work against me.

I kick wildly –
I am not ready to go.
There might be others like me.
Those men need to pay.

SHAME

I cough up water
On hands and knees,
Survival instincts kicking in.
I dig my fingers
Into the sand,
Trying to hold on –
Anything to feel
Something other than shame
Sizzling through my mind.

WHAT WERE YOU THINKING?

Do you know
How dangerous that was?

Do you have any idea
How scared I was?

More questions –
No answers.

I stare out the window,
Sadness boiling into anger.

I make a promise not to stop
Until those men pay.

ANGER

I'm angry at myself:
For not knowing better.
For not remembering.
For dragging everyone down.
For being afraid.
For not being stronger.
For allowing this to happen.

DARKNESS

Darkness is my best
   friend,
Hiding insecurity
   and fear.
It doesn't judge,

Darkness is my greatest
   enemy,
Amplifying insecurity
   and fear.
It doesn't help,

     Doesn't choose a side.

Darkness gives me space
To think and feel
In the safety

Darkness isolates me
Unable to feel safe
In the dangers

     Of my mind.

NEED TO KNOW

I tell Lau
It's important.

Something niggles
At the back of my mind:
I need to know.

Jackson hasn't called,
Hasn't asked how I am,
Hasn't acknowledged my existence.

Something isn't right:
I need to know.

ROLEX

Jackson's house –
Smaller than I remember.

Three bedrooms
In the heart of Greenview.

Jackson's mum –
Older than I remember.

Crow's feet
Frame her eyes.

She tries to stop me
But I push past.

My thoughts are frantic
As I race up the stairs.

I search his closet,
Take back my jumper.

A new Mac in the box
On his desk.

I open his drawers,
Clock the Rolex.

Heavy to hold –
It's not a fake.

It must have cost
5k easily.

Where did Jackson
Get that kind of cash?

MONEY

Jackson's mum is
A single parent,
Working two jobs
To pay the rent.

Jackson goes to school
Five miles from mine –
No time for a job
In his exam year.

So where did
The money come from?

WAS ANY OF IT REAL?

I met Jackson's mum
Two months ago.
Jackson and I kissed
In bed,
Limbs tangled.

His mum
Cooked Sunday roast –
Dry chicken,
Soggy potatoes,
Love enveloping
Her sons.

Jackson kissed my neck,
Squeezed my hand.
I smell his cologne
In the room,
Feel it crush the oxygen
From my lungs.

Was any of it real?

MEMORY III

I hit the ground,
Gravity dragging me down.

My head hangs heavy
As a door bangs shut.

Muddled words reach me:
Leave him.

Retreating footsteps –
Heavy and loud.

Something bright blinds me,
A noise – an engine? – purring.

I try to run,
Stumble over something.

Strong hands grab me,
Throwing me into the air.

I land with a *thud*,
As darkness folds in.

MEMORY

Memories collect information
About the world around us;
Process it,
Filter it,
File it away
Like a computer system.

I click on the memory
Of that night,
Waiting for it to load.
A dialogue box pops up:
Error message,
File *still* not found.

I REMEMBER

I remember:

The Spanish for candelabra:
El candelabro.

The first book I ever read:
The Gruffalo.

The last time I played football,
Torchlight following our movements.

My first time in hospital:
Tonsillitis when I was seven.

My first time swimming
In the wild Irish Sea.

I can remember things
From twelve years ago,
But I cannot remember
That night,
Haunting sleep,
Chilling consciousness.

OK

Mum and Dad call me
Into the kitchen.

I can tell by the frowns
This isn't good news.

They know about the trip to the seaside,
The one I made with Lau.
They're worried about me.

I scream through tears,
Knocking over a vase.

They want to know I'm OK.
I pray every night to be OK.

TEMPTATION

They call through the door,
Tempt me with dinner,
Offer me presents,
Promise me the world
If I come out.

I'm about to cave,
To unlock the door,
When I hear them
Talk about counselling.

I'M FINE

I'm not crazy,
Not someone
Needing to be locked up,
Not someone
Who can't function
Normally.

Why would I need counselling?
I'm doing fine.
I eat.
I drink.
I breathe.
I'm ~~not~~ fine.

I'M ~~NOT~~ FINE

I eat
~~When I have to.~~
I drink
~~When Mum watches me.~~
I breathe
~~Between nightmares.~~
I'm ~~not~~ fine.

FOR MY OWN GOOD

Dad took the key
From my bedroom door.

For my own good.

Mum passes my room
Glancing in routinely.

For my own good.

They give me a pocket alarm.

For my own good.

PRIDE

When I was twelve,
Mum took me to a colourful shop
In the middle of a shopping centre,
Helped me pick out iridescent wings
To wear to my first Pride parade.
She spent hours watching YouTube tutorials
So she could apply eye shadow
That resembled a beautiful rainbow.
She dusted glitter under my eyes.
When her parents disapproved,
She stood strong,
Challenged those around her,
Because I was her beautiful boy –
She'd do anything to see me happy.

COLOUR AND JOY

Mum knew before me
That I liked boys.
She took me to that parade
Before I told her
On my fifteenth birthday.
She showered me
In colour and joy,
Made sure that I knew
I was loved
Long before the world
Would judge me
For *who* I loved.

YOU CAN SHINE TOO

We saw a show
With dancers and singers –
My first time
Seeing a drag queen:
Ginger Snap.
She strutted across the stage
With the poise and confidence
Of a professional dancer,
Lip synced the words
With the raw emotion
Of an experienced singer.
She shone on stage,
In a ripple of sparkles and sequins.
At the end of the song,
She knelt down,
Held my hand in hers,
Whispered:
You can shine too.

FREE TO BE

Mum bought me
A rainbow–coloured feather boa
That snaked around me,
Keeping me warm,
Protecting me
From the awful things
People would say
Outside our sphere.

PITS OF HELL

A man held a microphone
On the street corner,
Heckling passers-by
Dressed in rainbow attire.
Citing Bible verses,
He scorned and shunned them,
Telling them they were going to Hell.

I heard Mum mutter:
With people like you
In the world,
Who needs Hell?

I asked her
If I was going to Hell.

She told me:
You're too pure
To belong
In the pits of Hell.

SNAP

Mum and I
Played card games
Every Sunday
Over hot chocolate and biscuits.
The sweet-cocoa smell
Enveloped us like a blanket
As we brought our hands
Down on the discarded pile,
Screaming SNAP
At the top of our lungs.

HOUSE OF CARDS

My life was a
House of cards –
Delicate,
Tentative,
Beautiful.
Ready to tumble
With the slightest breeze.

At school,
I tried to be normal,
To fit in,
But the house crumbled
Under an onslaught of slurs.
Every night I slept,
Quietly rebuilding the house,
Ready to be decimated
The next morning.

MARSHMALLOWS AND COCOA

Mum hands me a cup,
Mini marshmallows floating
In a sea of cocoa.

I enjoy a long sip,
Breathe in the intoxicating smell,
Slide the Post-it across the counter.

Mum unfolds it,
A smile for the first time
In months:

SNAP.

SWIMMING AGAINST THE TIDE

Mum always knew
The right words to say
To make everything better.

I don't want her to see me
Like this now –
Broken down and battered.

I don't want her to worry,
To bring her down with me –
Infecting everyone with my weakness.

I don't tell her how I feel
Like I'm forever swimming
Against the tide.

I don't want her to know.

THE TRUTH

I want the truth
About what happened
To me.

I want to know
Who they were,
Why they did it.

I want the truth
About Jackson –
What happened that night.

I want to know
About the Rolex
Weighing heavy by his bed.

I need to know.

SCOUR

I scour every social network,
Every article I can find.

I fall deep
Down a Reddit hole,
Scrutinising the threads
Knitting conversations together.

I HAVE QUESTIONS

I have questions
Left unanswered.
When I'm
At home,
At school,
At Lau's,
They stick to me
Like a second skin.

How do I fix this?

The police
Have all they need
To investigate.

Is this my fault?

The only thing
Left to do:
Wait.

Do I deserve this?

I have questions –
I need answers.

Why did this happen to me?

If I want answers,
I'll have to find them
Myself.

AFRAID

I'm afraid to sleep,
To see the figures
Tower over me.

They haunt me,
Never letting go.

I stare into the mirror,
Not recognising the figures
Hovering around me.

COUNSELLOR

The counsellor welcomes me,
Asks me open questions,
Scribbles notes
As she analyses every movement.

She gives me websites
I can look up,
Booklets that offer advice,
Exercises that will reduce my stress.

She doesn't reassure me
With false promises
Like everyone else.

She doesn't offer anything
She cannot deliver.

NORMAL BEHAVIOUR

It shouldn't come as a surprise
That she diagnoses me with
Anxiety disorder and PTSD.

Flashbacks are normal.
I'll have to be vigilant
To avoid this happening again.

This is normal behaviour
And it can be unlearned.

MEDICATED

Mum watches
As I place
White pills
On my tongue.

This is
My life now –
Being minded,
Being monitored,
Being medicated,
In hope
They can piece me
Back together again.

THE WEIGHT OF NOT KNOWING

When I'm alone,
Staring into the darkness,
My anger disappears,
My worries vanish.

Nothing bad ever happened
In my room.
Nothing can happen with
Mum helicoptering through the hall
Every half hour.

The only thing left is
A well of sadness that
Bubbles to the surface,
Drowning me in sorrow
Until tears run dry and
My body aches from
The weight of not knowing.

WHAT DID I DO ...?

I'm still mad at Lau.
He told my parents
I might be at risk,
That I swam out of view.

He's right,
But I fought
Against the waves,
Against the worry,
Against the weeds
Pushing through the cracks
Of my mind.

As angry as I am,
He's texted every day,
He took me to the hospital,
He held me tight
When the police
Asked question after question.

Where would I be
If it weren't for Lau?

WHY?

Jackson was everything
I never thought I would have.

Jackson was confident
When he swaggered up to me,
Asking me out at Onyx.

Jackson was kind
When he stayed up late
Listening to my troubles.

Jackson was my lifeline
When I felt scared –
Always saying the right things.

Jackson was my everything.
Why isn't he here
For me now?

REALITY

Loud crashing
Heavy breathing
Darkness suffocating
Covers binding
Light shining
Dad hovering
Grip sliding

On reality.

TRAPPED

Mum hovers around me.
Dad carries me to the bed.

Mum is crying.
Dad holds my hands.

Mum wants to know what happened.
Dad wants to know if I am OK.

I'm unable to speak,
Trapped in a nightmare.

TERROR

Night terrors –
They can strike
At any time.

Death–grip on mind,
They pull me in –
Spit me out
When I've fed them
My fears.

VENOM

It's always the same dream:
A giant snake,
Slithering after me,
Fangs bared
As it towers over me.
I trip,
Twist my ankle.
The snake attacks,
Swallowing me whole.

MY BODY

Sticky and hot –
My skin.

Wild and racing –
My mind.

Fine and functioning –
My organs.

Frozen –
My body.

CONTROL

Have you ever felt
Like you weren't in control –
A disconnect
Between mind and body?

Have you ever felt
Like you couldn't breathe,
Couldn't hear anything
Over your racing heart?

Have you ever woken
From a nightmare,
Unable to escape
Your darkest fears?

DOCTOR

I sit next to Mum,
Fingers intertwined with mine,
As we sit across
From the doctor.

I tell him what it was like –
To wake but not move,
To think but not feel,
To be but not breathe.

I tell him about my nightmare –
A snake sliding around me
Swallowing me whole.

Mum tells him about the screams,
But I do not remember screaming.

Mum tells him about the crash,
But I do not remember falling.

I tell him about the paralysis,
Coffin–still struggling for life.

SLEEP PARALYSIS

Sleep paralysis:

Caused by atonia –
Brief loss
Of muscle control.

Can cause hallucinations –
Bringing nightmares
To life.

Can be isolated
Or recurrent –
Which will it be
For me?

CONNECTED

Mum's hands are soft,
Conjuring comfort and discomfort –
Feelings born from that night.

I push down the discomfort,
Needing to be connected
To a place and person.

I need to feel connected.
I need to feel accepted.
I need to feel loved.

BROKEN

My mind is broken:
A sea of thoughts and feelings
Stirring beneath the surface.
I can't focus
On the here and the now
When the past
Weighs so heavily
On my mind.
It pulls at my thoughts,
Tears at my emotions,
Consumes me
Until it's an effort
To eat,
To sleep,
To breathe.

TOMORROW

Tomorrow is my first day
Back at school.
Nobody knows what happened
Except Lau.
How can I be expected
To go back to my old life
When the jigsaw piece I've become
No longer fits?

TIME FOR SCHOOL

The smells are the same –
It's me that's changed.

I linger at the entrance,
Students knocking my shoulders,
Breath trapped in my throat.

My hand shakes
As I place my fingers
On my locker.

A wave of nausea
Makes my knees buckle.

I try to focus,
Try to act normal.
No one can know
What happened.

I take the Post-it
Stuck to my locker,
Black dots filling my vision
As I read the words:
Is it true?

IS IT TRUE?

The three words
Ask a question
I cannot answer.

The words disappear
On my tongue.

I don't want
To be reminded
Of that night.

DENIAL

I shake my head,
Laugh at the idea,
Deflect and defend.

It works:
Belief shines bright
In their eyes ...

Until lunchtime.

BACK OF MY MIND

Somewhere in the back
Of my mind,
I want to be the me
Everyone used to see.

I want to be the me
That Jackson loved.
I want to glow all day
Without effort.

I don't want to know
The things I know.
I don't want to look
In the mirror
Because I know
What I will find.

@RUMOUR_HAS_IT

Jay Walker
Was drugged
And raped
Saturday night.

Woke up in a park,
No memory.
Went to hospital,
Spoke to police.

Maybe he deserved it?

SCRUTINY

My inbox blows up,
Mentions and tags
Increasing social currency,
But I do not want
This scrutiny.

They question me,
Judge me,
Demand proof
That I was …
That *it* happened.

The looks,
The whispers,
The silence
Filling the classroom
When I enter –
An overload of emotions.

@JAYWALKER2007

#IBelieveHim	#IDontBelieveHim
Why would he lie?	He's such a liar.
He's nothing to gain,	He loves attention.
I stand with him.	Where is the proof?

I DON'T WANT YOUR PITY

I don't want your sorrys,
Don't want your pity presents
Waiting to be unwrapped.

I don't want expectant looks
Offering support
I don't want or need.

I don't want that look
In your eyes
When you pass me in the halls.

I don't want it.
I don't need it.

OUT OF CONTROL

The bell rings –
Everyone leaves.
My hands grip
The table tightly.

If I let go,
Everything will spin
Out of control.
I bite my lip.

Staring ahead,
I ignore Mrs Suarez.
The blackboard text blurs
But I don't blink.

The words water
Under the weight
Of a future robbed.

TURN OFF THE LIGHT

When Mrs Suarez is gone,
I turn off the light,
Lay head to cool desk,
Praying this will end.

This has rippled
Into every part of my life,
I don't know
Who I am any more.

NOTHING MATTERS

The trees blur
Into nothingness.

I don't see the faces
Of parents pushing prams.

Everything looks small
From this window.

Mum zooms along,
Filling silence with idle chatter.

Nothing matters.

FUTURE

I wish I could forget,
Cut out the parts
Of my brain
Holding on to the echoes
Of an event
I can't recall.

If I could,
I'd roll up my sleeves,
Grip a scalpel tightly,
Slashing away at past Jay
To preserve my future.

HOW TO TRAIN YOUR MEMORY

There's no app or guidebook
To train your memory –
No answers to the questions
Playing on repeat.

Memory is not a dog
You can work with,
That you can reward
For a job well done.

It doesn't care
If you know or not.

MUTUAL GROUP SUPPORT

They say talking will help.
Lifting the lid
On Pandora's box –
Will that help anyone?
I cannot remember
The details of
That night.
How do these strangers
Expect me to talk?

A THOUSAND SADNESSES

Our collective trauma
Fills up this pastel room,
Bursting through window–pane cracks,
Shattering glass.

I cannot breathe with the weight
Of a thousand sadnesses
Choking the air from my lungs.

I'm on the floor.
Feeling so small,
I can almost see oxygen atoms
Escaping around me.

HEY

Hey, someone shouts.

The first time is
Always the worst.
You don't have to talk,
But if you want to ...

They hand me
A slip of paper:
Their number scrawled
In fill–the–page numbers.

See you next week.

They smile.
I practise a smile.
It feels strange.

THEIR NAME IS RAIN

They don't pry,
Don't expect me
To tell my story
When they tell theirs.

They don't
Pressure me
To be happy
Because it makes
Others comfortable.

They don't judge
Or show contempt
When I tell them
About that night,
Filling it with more detail
Than I've managed before.

NON-BINARY

Rain doesn't identify
As a girl
Or a boy.

They don't resonate
With she or he,
Him or her,
Hers or his.

Rain doesn't fit the mould.
Can't understand why it matters
What parts you have.

Rain's gender lives through them –
Some days,
They are resistant and rebellious;
Other days,
They want to wear combats and florals.
They see the rules,
They break the rules.

It's their journey,
Their life.

Rain is non-binary.

UNDERSTANDING

Rain was touched
By their father
Years ago.

They never told
Their mother
About it.

A year ago,
At a low point,
They felt crushed.

Anger floods
Their voice
When they speak of him.

He walks free.
Rain seethes –
A different person
When they speak his name.

POWER

There is power
In a name.

There is power
In speaking out.

There is power
In sharing secrets.

There is power
In Rain.

I WON'T BE THE LAST

I'm not the first
To be touched
Without consent

I won't be the first
To speak to police
About those nights.

I won't be the first
To ask myself
Is this my fault?

I won't be the last
To be hurt
Without consequence.

I won't be the last
To speak to doctors
About those scars.

I won't be the last
To feel like
This is my fault.

BREAK THE CYCLE

I want answers.
I *need* answers.
I must break the cycle,
End the victim line
With me.
I must make sure
They are punished.
I must make sure
No one feels the pain
I do.

TRIGGER MEMORIES

I read every article,
Scour every Reddit comment,
Listen to every TED talk
In hopes there is a way
To remember.

I scribble ideas,
Create a list
Of possibilities
That might trigger memories.

THE LIST

Let yourself write freely,
Without focus,
Without sleep,
In a trance.

Banish inhibitions.

Find peace with meditation –
Let your mind drift.

If all else fails –
Return to the scene
Of the crime.

WRITE

Write before coffee,
Write late at night
Before bed
When you're tired.
Write when sleep
Has its claws
Curling around your mind.
Write when you're vulnerable
And maybe,
Just *maybe*,
You'll remember.

TRANCE WRITING

I am at Onyx Bar
With Jackson.

He goes ████████
████████████████████
████████████████████

The car boot opens.
████████████ got out.
They took me
To ████████████

████████████████
██████████████████████
██████████████████████

████████████

I wake up
In the park.

MEDITATE

I press play,
Cross my legs,
Close my eyes.

I imagine myself
By the ocean,
Tasting salty air.

I dip my fingers
Into the water,
Focusing on my third eye.

My thoughts clear.
My senses withdraw.
A sentence forms.

I'LL BE RIGHT BACK

I'll be right back.

Jackson's last words.
I was in the alley.
He left me.

I'll be right back.

Where did he go?
Why did he leave?
How long was he gone?

I'll be right back.

What did he do
When he came back and
I was gone?

NEW MESSAGE

Hey,

Why did you leave me
In the alley alone?

What did you do
When you saw I was gone?

Why haven't you
Replied to my texts?

I HOPE YOU UNDERSTAND

I love you, Jay,
But this is too much.
I feel so guilty –
Trying to process it all.
I can't see you
Right now.

I hope you understand.

I DON'T UNDERSTAND

I don't understand:

How you can love someone
So much, but not text?

Why Jackson feels so guilty
If he did nothing wrong?

Why he didn't call someone
When he knew I was missing?

ONE THING

I've exhausted the list,
Deep-dived into the caverns
Of Reddit,
Tried every trick
In hopes that something –
A taste,
A smell,
A sound –
Will unlock my lost memories.

I scan the page
Of crossed-out ideas.
There's one left,
One idea that
Fills me with dread:
Return to the scene
Of the crime.

STRONG ENOUGH

I'm not strong enough
To do it alone.
If I tell Lau,
He'll tell my parents.
I cannot take
This next step.
Yet.

NO MEMORY

Just pain
Guilt rising
Shame boiling
Eyes scanning
All around
For signs
For comfort
For belonging
For anything.

THE ROCKY HORROR PICTURE SHOW

We were fifteen
When Lau and I
First saw
The Rocky Horror Picture Show.

I thought it was wonderful.
Lau thought it was weird
Until 'The Time Warp'
Sucked us both into the madness.

It became a Halloween tradition,
Reliving the magic
Dressed as our favourite characters –
Lau a predictable Brad,
Me an unpredictable Magenta.

THERE FOR YOU

I feel normal
Watching Lau roll
A gutterball.

Lau asks how I am,
As I eye the pins
Before me.

I feel so many things –
None of them are
Happiness.

We have good days.
We have bad days.
Whatever day it is,
I'll always be there
For you, Jay.

NOT THE ONLY ONE

Rain sent me an article
Published six months ago.
I scan the words,
Dread sinking in.

I'm not the only one
To wake up,
Not remember,
From a night
Spent in Onyx Bar.

There was another –
Guy or girl,
I do not know.
The article doesn't say.
How will I find them?

PART 3

Fuelling the Fire

I AM NOT …

I am not afraid.
I am not guilty.
I am not ashamed.

I am not afraid.
I am not guilty.
I am not ashamed.

I am not afraid.
I am not guilty
I am not ashamed.

But …

All I feel is fear.
All I hear is guilt.
All I know is shame.

DIARY

I start a diary
To capture
The day to day,
So I can cast out
Some of the shame.

My counsellor tells me
I should remember
Good times
From before,
Reminders that life
Can be good.

It's hard to focus.
Anger and sadness
War inside me.

Dear Diary ...

I don't know
Who I am
Any more.

I'm not strong enough
To return to Onyx,
But I need answers.

I need to know
Who did this to me.

How do I move on
If I never find them?

The pen rests on the page,
Ink bleeding my words
Into obscurity.

NOWHERE AND EVERYWHERE

I ride the bus
To nowhere and everywhere
When I need to think.

A man sits beside me,
Dark shades and a white stick,
Holding out a hand.

The warmth of his skin
Ignites something
Inside me.

I sit like that
Until the penultimate stop
When the man stands.

When he goes,
He leaves a warmth behind.

FOR EVER

I know this isn't for ever,
Not an eternal winter.
There are splashes of spring,
Swashes of summer,
Sprinkles of autumn
Waiting for me,
But am I strong enough
To make it?

WHEN THE WORLD SHAKES

Rain holds my hand
When the world shakes
Around me.

They keep the cracks
At bay
With bear-like hugs.

They never prod or probe,
Seeking the whens, the whats,
The whys and the hows.

Rain keeps me afloat
When social systems
Try to tear me down.

WISH

When I was seven,
Mum took me to the park,
Hoisted me into the air,
Spun me through
A sea of dandelion seeds.
We lay on the ground,
Arms stretched overhead,
Staring at white fluff
Swimming through crystal skies.

Make a wish,
She told me,
Holding out a dandelion.
Dandelions grant you one wish.
Close your eyes,
Blow the seeds.

I closed my eyes,
Wishing for a bike,
As bright and blue
As the sky.

BLUE BIKE

The garage door opens.
My bike glints
In the winter sun.

You don't always get
What you want
When you want.
I can't reach out,
Capture my memories
Like wild dandelion seeds
In tiny hands.

I can't cycle
Away from my problems,
But I can step into
A memory that is mine,
A memory that is welcome,
A memory that bears no harm.

DESIRES

Sitting is uncomfortable,
Cycling makes me ache,
But there's something so soothing
About cool air rustling hair and
Drizzle settling on soft skin.

I forget about the world,
Forget about the online bubble
Blowing up my inbox,
Blowing up my socials.

I cycle away from fears,
Power closer to desires.

REDDIT

Me: Looking for someone,
                       It happened to me too.

A day passes.

Me: I need to know.
                       I need answers.

Shy_Boi_2007:   Can we talk?

BLAME

I blamed myself for so long,
But someone did this to me.

I thought I got too drunk,
But I only had two beers.
Was I asking for it,
Wearing a crop top and shorts?

No.

None of this is true.
I did not deserve this.
I did not ask for this.
I did not want this.

I know this now.
For the first time in weeks,
My feelings are clear.
A fiery anger takes hold of me –
Will not be extinguished
Until I know who was responsible.

I WILL BE WATCHING

To whom it may concern,

You should be scared,
You should be worried.
Get used to looking
Over your shoulder.
I will be waiting,
I will be watching.

Yours,
Justice

NEED TO KNOW

Not a want –
But a need.

I need to know
Who did this.

I need to know
The whos,
The whys,
The whats.

I need to know
They will never
Do this again
To me,
To him,
To anyone.

SLEEP

Sleep never comes
When I want it to.

Sleep floats above,
Taunting me mercilessly.

Sleep never rests –
Neither do I.

Sleep knows I need it,
But it does not need me.

Sleep knows and deep down,
So do I.

BREAK THE SILENCE

Break the silence
Like one of Mum's prized vases.
Shatter it into a hundred pieces –
Each one
As sharp and sinister
As the next.

Don't cut yourself
On the broken shards
Of silence.

SAD SMILES

The officers greet me
With sad smiles.
They explain the samples
Don't match their records.

They are hopeful though –
Now they will widen the search,
Cast a wider net
To catch the man that
Did this to me.

INNOCENCE

They questioned Jackson,
Took samples –
No match.

I should be happy –
Jackson is innocent.

Jackson *is* innocent,
Isn't he?

BITTER TASTE

If Jackson is innocent,
Why does his name
Taste bitter in my mouth?

If Jackson is innocent,
Why does my vision blur
At the sound of his name?

If Jackson is innocent,
Why can't I look at pictures
Without falling apart?

If Jackson is innocent,
Why does every part of me
Refuse to believe it?

LOVE

Love isn't extravagant gifts,
Expensive meals,
Enchanting nights out.

Love is a bond
Of trust and passion,
Fused with a promise
To be there
For each other
In times of light or dark.

Love is giving all of yourself
Without reservation,
Diving into new territory,
Trusting that the other person
Feels the same.

Love is not
Something you can examine
Under a microscope,
Touch with your hands,
Pull close like the warm arms
Of a lover.

Love is magical.
Love isn't pain.
Were Jackson and I
Ever in love?

HEARTS

Love:
Four letters,
One syllable.

Love:
No test to take
To know it's real.

Love:
Unites countries,
Destroys empires,
Breaks hearts.

FIRST BOYFRIEND

I loved Jackson –
At least I thought I did.
My first boyfriend,
Leaning by the side of the stage
At Onyx.
Swigging a beer bottle,
His tattoo caught my eye –
Snake coiled,
Eating itself.
He strutted over,
Asked if I wanted to dance.
He told me everything
I wanted to hear,
Everything I needed to hear –
I drank it up with both hands.

IDEA OF A PERSON

Can you fall in love
With the idea of a person?

If they say
All the right things?

If they tell you
What you want to hear?

If they shower you
In adoration?

Can you fall in love
With the idea of a person

When they tell you
Vicious lies?

HOW TO FIX A HEART

Bandages and splints
Heal a broken arm.

Plasters and bandages
Help with cuts and gashes.

Scalpels and antiseptic
Help with infection.

What mends a broken heart?

HEAD AND HEART

Head and heart –
Both have had their fair share,
Bloodied and beaten,
Broken down into dust
By one boy.
Who knew one person
Could cause so much damage?

RAIN'S VERDICT

If he wasn't
Who he said he was,
The love was
Never real.

If he told you
Beautiful things,
Never meaning
The words he said,
He was a liar
With a dark heart.

If he's the reason
For the pain you feel,
He deserves to pay.

WHAT NOW?

Even if he didn't love me,
I had feelings for him.
I felt it,
Felt something –
Those feelings can't be a lie.
Can they?

I NEED TO KNOW

If Jackson had anything
To do with this
I need to know.

The Rolex weighs heavy
In my mind.

I need to know.

@SHY_BOI_2007

I tread carefully,
Understanding what it's like
To live with this pain
From the past.

I prod gently,
Knowing that if I push
Too far,
He'll end the chat.

I go slowly,
Because if Shy Boi disappears,
I have no chance
Of getting justice.

HAPPENED TO HIM TOO

It happened to him too
In the club.
He woke up in a park –
No memory
Of the night before.

He couldn't figure it out,
Remember how he got there,
What happened that night.

He had flashbacks,
But no places or faces.
He remembers the boy
He went clubbing with though.

TATTOO

The last thing he remembers:
Flashing lights near Onyx.

The last drink he had:
Vodka and coke –
Just one.

The last face he saw –
Dark hair and tall,
Tattoo of a snake
Eating itself
On his right arm.

LOTS OF PEOPLE

Lots of people have tattoos.
Lots of people like snakes.
Lots of people know about ouroboros.
Lots of people have dark hair.
Lots of people are tall.

Lots of people ...

LIES

He told me
I was his everything.

He told me
He loved me.

He told me
I didn't need to worry.

He told me
Lie after lie.

I sit replaying every memory,
Deciphering fact from fiction.

HE MUST KNOW

I suspected he wasn't innocent
But I did not expect this.

Two boys –
Same age,
Same club,
Same crime.

He told me I was special,
So very special,
But how can that be true
Knowing what I know?

The search shines a light
Into the dark corners
Of Jackson's past.
He might not have
Done the deed,
But he must know.

HORNETS' NEST

Lau pleads with me,
Not to poke
The hornets' nest
But they poked me first.

He begs me
To find another way,
To work with the police and
Find justice.

I consider it,
Think about all the things
My counsellor told me,
Fight against the darkness
Threatening to drown me.

1 IN 60

There's more of a chance
Of having food poisoning,
Losing something in the mail,
Living to 100,
Finding a coin on the pavement,
Than convicting the monsters
That left me like this.

GLASS BOY

The glass boy,
Composed of
Hope,
Anger,
Pain –
Heated to 1500 degrees,
Burning the ashes
Of a former self.
You see through him,
Transparent and shining,
But you do not know
What he's thinking,
What he's feeling.
Sharp–to–the–senses touch,
Capable of carving new paths
Into old bodies.
Shatter him
At your peril.

RAIN KNOWS

Rain understands –
Their father wasn't convicted.
He left bruised maps
Across their body,
Broke their nose,
Left them crying
In a pool of blood.

Now,
He has a new girlfriend,
A new house,
A new kid
On the way.

Rain knows
What it's like
To hurt,
To never truly heal –
They look whole
But when they talk,
I see the faint cracks
Where they've pieced themselves
Back together again.

TOGETHER

Rain's eyes darken
As they make the decision
To confront their father.

I don't tell Rain.
It's too much, too soon
For me.

I don't tell them
How scared I am
Because Rain's pain is my pain.

We're in this together.

DOES HE HURT YOU TOO?

Where are we?
I ask them.

Rain ignores me,
Marches past
The black Audi,
Across the manicured lawn,
Up to the door.

They smash
The brass knocker
Against dark wood.

A woman answers,
Her face a puzzle.
If Rain is shocked,
They don't show it.

Does he hurt you too?

The woman pulls her arm
To her chest,
But I see the bruises
Dotting her body.

Don't be scared,
Rain tells her.
You can end it.

Tears trickle
Down their cheeks,
Leaving mascara streaks.
The woman doesn't speak
As she closes the door.

Rain makes it to the gate
When they scream
At the full moon,
Howling fear and pain
From their body.

PAIN

I hold Rain as they cry,
Our pain welling
Into a cloud of crimson smoke that
Burns the oxygen
From our lungs.

It's too much for us to bear
But it will suffocate us
If we don't cry it
From our fragile bodies.

IN TWO MINDS

We can't.   We must.
It's not safe.   It'll never be safe.
Leave it.   Do it.
You can't undo this.   It's now or never.
Think about it.   Are you in?

DO I DARE?

My mind –
A cyclone
Of questions.

Should I?
Could I?
Can I?

What then?
Why now?
When?

Do I dare?
In a minute,
There is time
To take back mistakes
Yet to be made.

TRIED THEIR BEST

The officers have exhausted all options,
Pushed for a result
But the results were not there.

They tried their best –
Grim lines painted onto sombre faces
As they deliver the death blow.

No more suspects.
Nothing to prove it.
No more hope.

I am not the 1 in 60.

TRAPPED

Nothing lasts for ever,
Everyone keeps telling me.

Bruise–battered bodies
Heal.

Guilt–coated emotions
Fade.

Buzzing thoughts
Dissipate.

But *when* will this pass?

If nothing lasts for ever,
Four weeks on:
Why am I trapped?

FRIENDS

Lau and I
Have been friends
For two years.

Rain and I
Have been friends
For two weeks.

Lau means well
I know that
But he's not
What I need right now.

Rain helps me
I know that
And they're exactly
What I need right now.

NO MATTER THE COST

I am prepared to get answers
No matter the cost.

Rain understands my pain
In ways Lau never will.

Lau will never understand
Why I need to do this.

SCENE OF THE CRIME

Rain pretends it's their birthday,
Arriving at the front door
With dynamic energy,
Greeting Mum and Dad.

I am allowed
To celebrate with Rain.
To enjoy a night off
Of parental monitoring.

I told Rain about Jackson,
All the times I have tried
To reclaim memories
From that night.

Tonight:
I return
To the scene of the crime.
Tonight:
I return to Onyx.

DISGUISE

Rain says
The makeup will disguise
Our faces,
Make it easier
To gain admission
To Onyx.

They smear foundation
Onto my face.

The theme for tonight's party:
Circus Berserkus.

Rain runs brushes
Over nose and mouth.

They dust my face
With powders.

I stare into the mirror,
At the face that is not mine.

The club-kid beat
Re-shapes my face,
Accentuating features
I never knew I had.

WE WAIT

They barely check the fake IDs
As they usher us
Inside the cavernous club.

The lights blind me,
The beats pounding,
Matching my heart.

My senses are alight,
Pulled in all directions,
As I navigate the club.

Rain finds an alcove,
Where we can see
But not be seen.

We sip our drinks.
We wait.

FIRST SIGHT

I spot Jackson,
Dressed smart-casual
With a boy
I don't recognise.

My heart races
As they melt into the crowd.

I follow,
My body puppeteered
Through winding beats and
Sweating bodies.

Jackson returns,
Marching away
From the fire-exit door,
Without the boy.

I burst through the door,
Into the dimly lit alley.

I run to the boy,
Pull him by his hoodie.

What the hell?
He snaps.

He's peeing,
His eyes sharp and searching.

The gays in this city are
So damn weird.
Should've stayed in London.

He shrugs,
Disappears into the darkness,
Leaving me
With the shadows
Of my past.

I WAS WRONG

I was wrong.
I was wrong.

Maybe I was wrong
About Jackson too?

I was wrong.

Press hands to head,
Push thoughts back inside.

Body to ground,
Hands searching.

Tears staining cheeks.

I'm not me,
Not here.

I was wrong.

MISSED THE JUMP

Rain finds me on the ground,
Belly to concrete,
Arms spread wide
Like a bird that missed the jump.

Rain scoops me up,
Shoulders my weight,
Guides me to the safety
Of my house.

PICK–POCKET

Rain pick–pocketed
Jackson's phone.
They hand it to me,
Big eyes burning.

What could his phone
Possibly reveal
That tonight couldn't?

Rain asks for his PIN:
I do not know.

1234
Four attempts left.

4321
Three attempts left.

Jackson's birthday:
7 July.

0707
Two attempts left.

0000
One attempt left.

Rain urges me to think,
To take a moment.

Jackson's house number,
Wooden digits painted blood red.
Would he be so careless?

I tap the code with jelly fingers:
1902.

I hold my breath:
We're in.

The weight
Of Jackson's guilt
Fills my room,
Smothering us.

BREATHE

If I am fuel,
Rain is fire –
Perfect balance
Of heat, oxygen and fuel.

I'm missing elements,
Missing parts
That make me whole.

Rain's kindness
Fills me with heat –
All I need now:
Oxygen.

Breathe.

AT WAR WITH MYSELF

He loved me
He bought me presents
He took me out
He was my boyfriend
He broke me.

He never loved you
He bought your body
He sold you out
He broke your trust
He broke you.

WRITING ON THE WALL

It should be easy:
Jackson drugged me,
Handed me over
To a pack of wolves.

Six men
Taking turns,
Like I was a game
They'd already won.

Six men,
Beating me,
Bruising me,
Breaking me.

Six men
Penetrating me.
I read the messages
As the light leaves my eyes.

OWN THE WORDS

I embrace the pain,
Let the anger boil,
Bubbling over my skin
Like acid.

It's taken weeks
For me to say,
To own the words.

They raped me.

HEART OF GLASS

I will find the men
Who did this to me.
My heart of glass
Will shatter
When I see them.
I will catch the shards and
Hurt them,
Just as they've hurt me.
They will bleed.
I will crush them
With clenched fists.

THROW AWAY THE KEY

I go to the support group.
I need my parents
To think I'm OK,
That everything is fine.
If they could peer
Inside my head,
They'd lock me up and
Throw away the key.

I WAS RAPED

Everyone watches me,
Waiting for my answer.

I never speak much
At the group sessions.

Rain reaches out,
Their hand squeezing mine.

I stare at the ceiling,
Searching for divine courage.

My breaths fill
The room to capacity.

Tears trickle down my cheeks
A slow yet steady stream.

I was raped.

RAPE

Rape is scooping out
Somebody's essence,
Leaving them hollow and hurt,
Wondering who they are,
What they did to deserve it.

Rape is a violation
Of trust and respect,
Intertwined with threats of violence,
Leaving questions
Without answers.

Rape is the worst thing
You can do to a person,
Before and after –
Forever in opposition.

SPEAKING MY TRUTH

Everyone snaps,
Clicks their fingers.
We do not touch or hug
In these sessions.
Touch is a trigger
For most of us.
I bathe in the recognition,
Acknowledge the achievement
Of speaking my truth.

UNSPOKEN WORDS

Rain and I
Have not spoken
In two days.

They catch me outside,
Admiration shining
In their eyes.

Unspoken words
Hang between us –
Rain speaks the unspoken.

FIGHT

Rain thinks
We should
Show the police.

If Jackson is convicted –
A pretty big IF –
He'll spend
Four,
Maybe five years
In jail.

He broke me –
I pick up a shard
Of my former self.
Time to fight back.

HOW CAN I BE SURE?

Let's say I hand the phone
To the police –
Jackson has skirted blame before –
How can I be sure
He won't this time?

We can cast the net
But Jackson will
Wriggle out of it.
There is only one way
I can be sure
He pays.

TWO MONTHS AGO …

Two months ago,
I was at Jackson's house,
Lying on his bed,
Kisses running down my neck.

Two months ago,
I was whole,
Head and heart
Healthy and strong.

Two months ago,
I was untouchable,
Buoyed by a love
I couldn't describe.

Today,
Jackson's lights are off,
The small window open
Just a crack.

I reach in,
Drop the letter,
Power surging through me.

LETTER

Meet at the Lakeside Café,
In the park,
Tomorrow at midnight.
Or I hand your phone
To the police.

REFLECTION

Sitting at my desk,
I stare into the mirror,
Wondering what Jackson
Saw in me,
What made me so easy
To exploit?
Was it my kindness?
Was I naïve?
Was I desperate for love?
I knew Jackson had secrets
But not ones like these.
I didn't think he would
Sell me out.
I try to forgive –
I want to forget –
But Jackson has no remorse.
Otherwise he wouldn't
Have told the world
About what happened.

SOCIAL BUBBLES

I was getting close
To the truth.
Jackson was interviewed
During my first day
Back at school.
He needed a diversion,
Something to deflect attention.
He told the world
I was raped.
@Rumour_Has_It –
An account run by Jackson.
He marked me out
As a target
For strangers
To jeer at and judge –
Taking my anonymity,
Shining a spotlight,
Bursting my bubble.

A POUND OF WORDS

Forgiveness is easy   Forgetting is hard
        Neither is easy for me
I can't forgive   I can't forget
        Until I get justice
He must feel   He will know
        The weight of his words.

ROSES

Mum is in the garden,
Planting roses by the fence.

I bend down,
Place my hand on hers.

She looks at me,
A smile in her eyes.

We don't need to speak –
Mum understands.

I pick up a rose,
Prick myself on the thorns.

Mum goes into the kitchen,
Fetching a plaster.

I watch as blood drips,
Disappearing on red petals.

MENDING THE CRACKS

I make two cups
Of hot chocolate,
Filled half with cocoa,
Half with marshmallows.

A sprinkle of cinnamon and
They're ready to go.

Mum is curled up
On the couch,
Legs tucked underneath her.

I hand her a cup,
Sit down beside her,
Smiling when she slides
An arm around me,
Pulling me close.

I wish I could bottle
This feeling,
Drink deep when nightmares
Come calling.

I close my eyes,
Bathe in the moment
Before I confront Jackson.

HEAL

I might never heal,
Never be whole,
But I can enjoy
The here and now.
Mum knows everything –
No reason to keep
Our distance
When I might never
Get this chance again.

A HUNDRED REFLECTIONS

I take the mirror
Off the wall,
Placing it on the bed.

I curl my hoodie
Around my fist,
Smashing the mirror
Into a hundred reflections.

A jagged piece calls to me,
I pocket it.
I am ready.

WISH

I wish I was a better friend
To Lau,
To Rain.

I wish I'd taken more time
To give rather than take
From Lau.

I wish I had more time
To capture the joy
Between our moments of grief.

I wish I could change
What happened to me,
But I can't.

This is how it must be.

THE TRUTH

I send them texts,
Thank them for all
They have given me.

I apologise for dragging them
Into this web
Of Jackson's design.

I tell them
The world will know the truth
By midnight.

THE GREAT ESCAPE

Dad works shifts.
It will be morning time
Before he notices
I am missing.

When Mum is asleep,
I climb out of my window,
Using the trellis
To lower myself.

I stare back
At my house,
Wondering what they'll think
When morning arrives.

LAKESIDE CAFÉ

It takes two trams
To get to the Lakeside Café.
I pull the drawstrings
Of my hoodie
Closer to my face,
Watching people
Ready for a night
On the town.
I was like them once,
Excited to dance
My worries away.
I stare out the window,
Wishing I could go back
To that time.

READY

I reach down,
Touching each blade of grass
With my fingertips.
I stare up at the stars
Winking at me
In the ominous sky.
I splash my hands
In the lake,
Relishing every sensation.

I should be scared
But I'm not.

I'm ready for this
To be over.

AM I READY TO DO THIS?

Someone casts shadows
As they approach.
I grip the shard tightly,
Ready to get justice,
Ready for the end.
Memory fragments
Overwhelm me.
The shard trembles –
Am I ready to do this?

MOONLIGHT

Jackson watches me warily,
Tells me it's all a misunderstanding.

Jackson steps cautiously closer,
Says that it's all OK.

Jackson reaches out to me,
Asks for the phone.

Jackson lunges at me,
Demands the phone.

OUR LOVE WAS NEVER REAL

Why?

He did it for his mother,
So they could move
Somewhere nice,
Away from the violence
On their estate.
He did it for his little brother,
To give him a proper chance
At life.

How many?

Three,
Including me.

I don't believe him.
I found the Rolex.

How many?

He doesn't know.
At least he's honest
This time.

Did you ever love me?

He tells me he did –
Not at first –
But in the end.
He felt bad.

His hands are shaking,
Eyes darting,
Hands fidgeting.

I remember what Rain told me:
If he's the reason
For the pain you feel,
He deserves to pay.

I let the words sink in –
Our love was never real.

FIVE BREATHS

Five breaths
To reassess the situation.

Jackson sold me out.
Manipulated me.
Packed me off to those predators –
For a payday.

He deserves this.
I need this.

Five breaths
To reassess the situation.

BEG

He tells me he's sorry,
Begs for his life,
Another chance
To make things right.

Where was my chance?

I eye him cautiously,
Expecting him
To lunge again
At any moment.

His eyes aren't sorry though.
His body is heavy and stubborn,
Defying the words
Spewing from his mouth.

It doesn't take away the pain,
The memories fizzing
Inside my head.
He has no idea.

He's taken my essence,
Turned it into something
Dark and deadly.

The shard weighs heavy.
Jackson is all pleases and don'ts
But he knows what he's done,
He needs to face it.

I don't want to be here –
Don't want the pain,
The nightmares that paralyse
On late, long nights.

If I do this,
Am I any better than him?
Than the men who used me and
Dumped me in the park?

Jackson moves closer –
I tell him to stop.
He strikes out –

INTERVENTION

A car races
Across the grass,
Horn blaring,
Lights flashing.
Lau parks the car,
Opens the door,
Pleads with me.
I glimpse Rain,
Squished into
The passenger seat.
Stop,
This isn't you.

FIGHT FOR LIFE

Jackson knocks me
To the ground.
He's on top of me,
Wrestling for control.
The shard flies
From my hand.
Jackson's nails are tiny teeth,
Needling my arms,
Breaking skin.
Lau is behind him
But Jackson is nimble,
Knocking him to the ground.
I wrench left and right,
Throw my weight
At him.
Our heads collide –
Jackson reels.
He's on his feet –
I barrel forwards
While he's off-balance.
I fight for my family.
I fight for my friends.
I fight for my life.

I fight for myself.

SURVIVAL

Something clicks inside me.
I've been so focused
On finding the answers,
Trekking a treacherous path
Without thought.
Guided by the fiery flames
Of my rage,
I've gotten what I wanted,
What I *thought* I wanted,
But I'm going to survive.
I want to live.

PROGRESS

I see the shard
At the edge
Of the lake.
My heart *thwump thwump thwumps*
In my chest –
I fumble for the shard.
I feel the anger,
The sadness,
The fear,
Spiralling out of me.
I know this isn't the end.
I know there are more
Who must pay
For what they've done,
But it's a start.

DESTROYING THE EVIDENCE

Jackson dives,
Knocks me down.
His hands search my pockets.
A memory flashes
Before my eyes.
I push it away
In time to see
Jackson scrambling
On hands and knees,
Launching the phone
Into the pond.
I watch my only evidence,
The pond swallowing
All traces of its existence.

PROOF

after everything
i am here
again
nothing to show
heart racing
palms sweaty
mind restless
jagged words
from Jackson's lips:
How you gonna
Prove it now?

I SEE RED

Jackson plucks the shard
From the grass.
Rain moves closer,
Helping me to my feet.

A police car
Screeches across park paths
Towards us.

I copied it to my drive.
As blue and red lights
Flash across the lake,
Rain smirks.
How you gonna
Prove it now?

Lau pushes me
Out of the way
As Jackson attacks,
Driving the shard
Into Lau's chest.
Through the blue lights,
I see red.

INSTINCT

something possesses me
takes over
disarms him
kicks him
scratches
punches
on top of him
seeing fear
seeing pain
seeing sadness
stepping back
looking down
breathing in
watching the shell
a boy
crack before me
creature shrivelling
into nothingness

FOCUS

Rain presses their jacket
To Lau's wound.
Lights flash around us.
Officers shout.
Rain screams.
I focus
On Lau,
Holding his hand,
Talking nonsense,
Keeping him awake.
He can't go like this.

PART 4

Justice

ALL I NEED

Jackson missed Lau's heart
By an inch.
He'll need plenty of bedrest
But he'll make
A full recovery.

I watch him sleeping,
In the bed –
Can't help thinking:
That should be me.

Lau opens his eyes.
Hey, he says.
Hey, I reply.
My mind is spiralling
Trying to process everything
But right now,
Sitting next to Lau
In amicable silence is
All I need.

HOSPITAL

From the hospital bed,
Lau asks me
Not to shut him out.
He has my best interests
At heart.
I know this now,
But at the time,
I wanted revenge.
I wanted the pain
To go away,
But I went about it
The wrong way.
What would have happened
If Lau didn't stop me?
What would have happened
If Rain didn't back up the messages?
Tears burst from my eyes –
It's over.
It's finally over.

BACK-UP

Rain backed up the messages,
On their drive.
They handed it to the police
When Lau figured out
Where I would go.
He remembered
My first date with Jackson –
A picnic by the lake
At the park.

MEMORY

I sit on the swing,
Lift my feet off the ground.
I can't stop thinking about Jackson.
When he touched me,
Snatched the phone from my pocket,
It triggered a memory.
I'm not sure if I saw everything,
But I saw enough.
I remember
How I got the bruises.
I remember
How they made me bleed.
I remember so much more
But still,
I'm not sure
If I know everything.
Right now,
I do not want to know.

THE SMALL THINGS

A week has passed –
Lau, Rain and I
Hold hands
On the playground swings.
I feel their warmth,
Their skin touching mine,
Reminding me
Of what I have.
We don't need to talk,
But I know if I need to,
Both of them will listen.
I relish the small things:
Walking in nature,
Movies with Mum,
Bowling nights with Lau and Rain.
It takes my mind
Off the uncertainties
Of the police investigation.

DECEIT

I contemplate writing a message
On social media,
On speaking out
Against the rumours.
That all came from Jackson though –
If they believe him,
If they run with his vitriol,
They're no better than the boy
Awaiting his fate
Behind bars.

MY VOICE

It's the first time –

I can sit with the group,
Not feel the silence scorch me
Like an exploding grenade.

The shackles of the past remain
But I can speak my mind
Clearly and confidently.

I've found my voice.
No one will take that
From me.

MAGIC

I curl up on the couch
Beside Mum,
Watching the bursts of snow
Blowing through our garden.
It disguises the weeds and cracked pavement
In a blanket of delicate white.
Cups to lips,
We drink in silence,
Acknowledging this marvel.
Mum pulls me closer.
Tomorrow,
A decision will be made.
Tomorrow,
I will know.

CHARGES

Jackson has been charged
With trafficking and aggravated assault.

He has pleaded
Not guilty.

His case will go to trial
On 1 April.

I hope I never see
His face again.

I WANT TO LIVE

There are moments of peace
Where I don't think about
The awful things they did
To me.

There are times of joy
When I cook with Mum,
Chit-chat with Rain and Lau
About everything and nothing.

But just like everything
There are flashes of pain
When I relive it all and
The pain crushes me.

I don't know if it's for ever
But it's my reality.
This won't be easy
But I want to live.

If you have experienced anything like the issues discussed in this book yourself, or you know somebody who needs help, you can talk to your doctor or practice nurse at your local surgery or seek help from a range of voluntary organisations including:

IN IRELAND

Rape Crisis Network Ireland
https://www.rcni.ie/

One in Four
https://www.oneinfour.ie/

Connect
https://connectcounselling.ie/

You can call 1800 77 88 88 (24-hour helpline) to get support from the Rape Crisis Centre in Ireland.

IN THE UK

Male Survivors Partnership
https://malesurvivor.co.uk/

Rape Crisis
https://rapecrisis.org.uk/

Women's Aid
https://www.womensaid.org.uk/

Victim Support
https://www.victimsupport.org.uk/

The Survivors Trust
https://www.thesurvivorstrust.org/

You can also access help from the 24-hour freephone National Domestic Abuse Helpline in the UK, run by Refuge, on 0808 2000 247.

IN THE US

Rape, Abuse & Incest National Network (RAINN)
https://www.rainn.org/

Call 800.656.HOPE (4673) to be connected with a trained staff member from a sexual assault service provider in your area.

In an emergency, call emergency services.

ACKNOWLEDGEMENTS

I want to thank my family for their moral support with all of my books, particularly my mam who encouraged me to follow my dreams. I wouldn't be half the writer I am today without my best friend, Jake. To the amazing team at Little Island Books – Matthew, Siobhán, Kate and Elizabeth – thank you for taking in my book and turning it into something special. Thank you to Jack for creating a vibrant, powerful cover that perfectly captures the essence of Trigger. A huge thanks to my friends – Eve, Yvonne, Kathleen, Ross and Hamish. Also thanks to my writing friends – Kate (for the morning writing sprints!), Liz Corr and Sue Wallman. Thank you to all of the schools that have supported me (especially Amy McKay) and shared lovely messages about my books and how they have impacted upon your students. Most importantly, thank you to the readers for reading my books and allowing me to share the thing I love most in the world.

Special thanks to Neil Dunnicliffe and Chloe Seagar for helping to make this book as strong as it can be.

The Eternal Return of Clara Hart

by Louise Finch

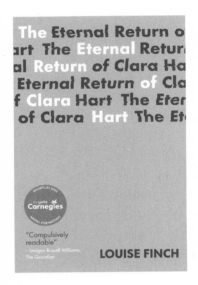

A sensational YA debut about toxic masculinity and gendered violence.

Wake up. Friday. Clara Hart hits my car. Go to class. Anthony rates the girls. House party. Anthony goes upstairs with Clara. Drink. Clara dies. Wake up. Friday again. Clara Hart hits my car. Why can't I break this loop?

A flicker in the fabric of time gives Spence a second chance. And a third. How many times will he watch the same girl die?

Praise for *The Eternal Return of Clara Hart*

"Compulsively readable"
– *The Guardian*

"I am glad this superb book exists"
– *The Irish Times*

"A devastating, essential journey"
– *Kirkus*, starred review

"Bold and honest"
– *The National*

Awards

Shortlisted for the Yoto Carnegie Medal for Writing 2023

Shortlisted for the Branford Boase Award 2023

Shortlisted for the Great Reads Award 2023

Shortlisted for the Badger Book Award 2023

Shortlisted for the YA Book Prize 2023

GRAPEFRUIT MOON

by Shirley-Anne McMillan

How far would you go to fit in?

Wealthy, popular Charlotte and quiet Drew from the council estate don't have much in common. Except for Adam — Charlotte's ex and leader of the toxic Stewards club.

As Drew struggles to follow the Stewards' rules, Adam is terrorising Charlotte with a video of them having sex.

A trip to Spain, poetry slams and a drag queen bring Charlotte and Drew closer together — and push them further than ever from who they used to be.

"Emotional, gripping, and so, so real"

Louise Finch, author of
The Eternal Return of Clara Hart

ABOUT LITTLE ISLAND

Little Island is an award-winning independent Irish publisher of books for young readers, founded in 2010 by Ireland's first Laureate na nÓg (children's laureate), Siobhán Parkinson. Little Island books are found throughout Ireland, the UK, North America, and in translation around the world. You can find out more at littleisland.ie

RECENT AWARDS FOR LITTLE ISLAND BOOKS

Youth Libraries Group Publisher of the Year 2023

IBBY Honour List 2024
The Táin by Alan Titley, illus. by Eoin Coveney
Things I Know by Helena Close

An Post Irish Book Awards:
Teen and YA Book of the Year 2023
Black and Irish: Legends, Trailblazers & Everyday Heroes by Leon Diop and Briana Fitzsimons, illus. by Jessica Louis

An Post Irish Book Awards:
Children's Book of the Year (Senior) 2023
I Am the Wind: Irish Poems for Children Everywhere ed. by Sarah Webb and Lucinda Jacob, illus. by Ashwin Chacko

White Raven Award 2023
Carnegie Medal for Writing shortlist 2023
YA Book Prize shortlist 2023
Kirkus Prize finalist 2023
The Eternal Return of Clara Hart by Louise Finch

Literacy Association of Ireland Biennial Book Awards:
Age 10–13 Award 2023
USBBY Outstanding International Books List 2023
Spark! School Book Award: Fiction Age 9+ Award 2022
Wolfstongue by Sam Thompson, illus. by Anna Tromop

Little Island
Books create waves